CONCEPTUALISED & WRITTEN BY: RAGHU SAWHNEY

ILLUSTRATIONS: PUSHPA GANDHRE

EDITING: RAHUL SAWHNEY

# The legend of Tooth Fairy

*This book belongs to:*

_____

_____

## RAGHU SAWHNEY

Once upon a time, in the Fairyland high up in the sky, lived a young fairy.

Her mother was the queen of the Fairyland and since she was the youngest fairy of the Fairyland, the other fairies lovingly called her Tanya.

As Tanya had no brothers or sisters of her own to play with, she used to fly down to earth to watch little children play. Tanya was very fond of little children.

Every time a little child got hurt and started crying, Fairy Tanya would start crying herself. And children would wonder why they heard two crying voices when only one child was hurt.

Soon Tanya grew up. Like all fairies, she had much work to do in Fairyland. She was given the task of looking after the beautiful lawns, gardens and fountains of the queen's palace.

This kept Tanya very busy indeed. Though she enjoyed the work given to her, she very much missed the sight of little children of earth and longed to see them.

One evening, when Tanya had finished her work in the Fairyland, she decided to visit earth! Off she went to earth, taking with her a box of sweets to munch on.

By the time she reached earth, it was late and most children had gone to bed.

But one little boy was awake and crying because he had broken his tooth. The little boy's parents consoled him. They told him that a new tooth would soon grow and everything would be all right.

But the boy refused to throw away his old tooth. He washed it carefully, dried it with his towel, and went to bed, holding the tooth in his little fist.

As soon as the boy fell asleep, his fist opened and the tooth fell out of his hand and rolled near his pillow.

Fairy Tanya was watching all this and was very sad for the boy. She was sure that when the boy woke up in the morning, he would be sad again because of his broken tooth.

She decided to take the tooth away and leave the box of sweets she had brought along in its place.

She kept the box under the boy's pillow and off she flew to Fairyland!

By the time she reached Fairyland, it was morning. Upon entering her house she met the Fairy Queen Mother who asked her where she had been. Tanya told her all about the little boy and his broken tooth.

Upon hearing the story, the Fairy Queen Mother was very worried and she immediately called a meeting of all the fairies.

She announced that what Tanya had done was a serious matter indeed.

She said, "This is the first time any fairy has left evidence of fairies for earth people to see. Now the people on earth will know that there are fairies living up in the sky".

She further added, "The biggest problem is that the boy who got the gift will tell all his friends and now every child who breaks a tooth will expect a present".

After a lot of discussion, it was decided that for the happiness of children on earth, what Fairy Tanya had started had to be continued.

Tanya was called to the meeting and told that from today, it would be her duty to visit earth every evening and give any child who had kept a broken tooth under their pillow, a present.

From that day, Fairy Tanya was called Tooth Fairy.

In the meantime on earth, when the young boy woke up, he started searching for his broken tooth. When he looked under his pillow, he found the lovely box of sweets! He had never seen a box as beautiful as this. The box had lovely flowers painted on it and its delicious smell filled the entire room. He quickly took a sweet out of the box and ate it.

He had never eaten such a delicious sweet! He ran to his parents' room and showed them the box. They were surprised too and wondered where the box came from.

When the boy went to school, he took the box along. He told all his friends about his broken tooth and the lovely box of sweets that appeared in its place in the morning.

Soon the whole school was talking about it.

All the children were sure that some kind fairy had taken the tooth and left the box of sweets behind. They all decided that, when their tooth broke, they too would keep their broken tooth under their pillow to see if they get presents in return.

The next day, a little girl from the school broke her tooth. She kept the tooth under her pillow and went to bed.

In the morning, there it was... a lovely little golden charm in the shape of a butterfly! Next to it was piece of pink note paper on which was written in gold ink –

*"With love from T.F."*

(T.F. stood for Tooth Fairy, of course!)

The news of a second child getting a present spread like wild-fire and soon the whole city knew about it. Now, children were very excited, looking forward to a gift when their tooth broke.

The next day another child got a present and then another and another and another!

Now children knew that there was indeed a Tooth Fairy who loved them very much! Every time their tooth broke, they knew, she would leave behind a lovely present so that they would forget about their pain and be happy as children should always be!

And now the Tooth Fairy had a lot of work to do! During the day she had to make lots of presents. Some presents she and her team made in the Fairyland, and some she bought from the best of shops on earth. And the night of course, was the busiest time, visiting earth to leave presents for children who had broken their tooth. It was a lot of work, but the Tooth Fairy loved it!

The Tooth Fairy chose the presents carefully for each child. And she would often go back to see if the children were happy with the presents she had given them.

One night when the Tooth Fairy was on her visit to earth, she came across a very pretty house. As she entered the house, she saw a little girl sleeping peacefully. The girl had golden hair and was wearing a pretty green nightgown. And when the Tooth Fairy felt under the pillow, there it was, a broken tooth!

The Tooth Fairy really liked the girl and decided to give her one of her best presents: a lovely white party dress with golden embroidery. The Tooth Fairy was sure the girl would look lovely in the dress.

The next day, the Tooth Fairy come back to see if the girl had liked her present. She was amazed to find that the girl had repacked the present and had kept it near the pillow. Next to the present was a note, which read:
"Dear Tooth Fairy,
Thank you very much for your present,
but I don't want it. Please return my tooth".
- Julie.

The Tooth Fairy was very puzzled. She thought may be Julie did not want a dress. So she took back the dress and in its place she left behind a silver necklace with pearls and a matching bracelet.
The Tooth Fairy was sure Julie would like the new present.

The next day when the Tooth Fairy came back, she was stunned to see that Julie had not even opened the present! Again, there was a note which said:
"Dear Tooth Fairy,
Thank you for giving me a new present, but I don't want it.
Please return my tooth". – Julie.

Now Tooth Fairy was very confused. She thought may be Julie did not want an expensive present. So she decided to leave behind an ordinary doll, hoping she would like the present this time.

But the next day when the Tooth Fairy went to see Julie, the present was again kept near the pillow with a similar note. This time, the Tooth Fairy did not know what to do. She was sure Julie wanted a present because she had kept the broken tooth under the pillow, but what was this special present that she desired?

So, Tooth Fairy took the present back and returned to the Fairyland.

She was upset because she knew Julie was unhappy at not receiving the present she wanted. But, more than that, the Tooth Fairy did not know how to solve this puzzle. Finally she decided to ask the Fairy Queen Mother to help her.

The Fairy Queen Mother was also very puzzled. She agreed with Tooth Fairy that Julie wanted a present but she too did not know what that present was.

So she asked Tooth Fairy to go to earth in the afternoon and make friends with Julie by becoming a little girl herself.

Off the Tooth Fairy went, and when Julie came to the garden to play, Tooth Fairy was there in the form of a girl! The two girls started playing together and soon became friends.

While they were playing, Julie saw that Tooth Fairy was wearing a very pretty necklace.

She asked the Tooth Fairy where had she purchased it from. The Tooth Fairy replied that some days back she had broken her tooth and she got it as a present from the Tooth Fairy. Then she asked Julie if she had ever got a present from the Tooth Fairy.

Julie replied very sadly, "Yes. A few days back I broke my tooth and the Tooth Fairy gave me a lovely white party dress. The dress was so beautiful that I really wanted to keep it, but I had to return it".

"Why"? exclaimed the Tooth Fairy.

"Because I know that my parents can afford to buy me a new dress, but what about other poor children who don't even have money to eat food. The Tooth Fairy has never given them any presents, so why should I take a present from the Tooth Fairy"?, Julie replied.

The Tooth Fairy was very upset on hearing this and said, "that's not true! Tooth Fairy does give presents to poor children as well".

With tears in her eyes, the girl replied, "No, she does not! I have a friend who lives in a broken hut. She is so poor, she doesn't have a single dress which is not torn. Her mother is dead and her father comes home drunk and beats her everyday. The other night he had beaten her so badly that she broke so many of her teeth. Even till today she is so sick that she can't get up from the bed. But, the cruel Tooth Fairy did not give her a single present. How then, could I accept that pretty dress from the Tooth Fairy?"

By this time, the Tooth Fairy was openly crying with grief, listening to the pain and suffering of the poor girl.

She felt so guilty that for a few moments she could not speak at all.

Finally she said, "Please take me to your friend's house. I must meet her".

Julie was very surprised to hear this, but agreed to take the Tooth Fairy to her friend's house.

When they reached the poor girl's hut, they saw that she was lying on the bed and was in great pain.

The Tooth Fairy asked Julie to go and fetch some water.

When Julie left to get the water, the Tooth Fairy gently patted the girl with her magic hands and cast a healing spell on the girl and her hut.

The poor girl's body healed immediately, her torn dress became a beautiful gown and, in place of the broken hut, there now stood a nice cottage surrounded by flowers!

By the time the poor girl opened her eyes, the Tooth Fairy had disappeared!

When Julie returned to the hut with water, she was surprised to see the new cottage and when she saw that her friend was well, she was overcome with joy.

She knew that the girl that she had brought to the hut was none other than the Tooth Fairy herself !

Lying on the cot was a note:

*" Thank you for giving me your precious gift ".*

T. F.

*The End*